For my mum, Jude,
a very wonderful cheerer-upper

First U.S. edition 2013

Library of Congress Catalog Card Number 2012950626

ISBN 978-0-7636-6657-6

13 14 15 16 17 18 TLF 10 9 8 7 6 5 4 3 2 1

Printed in Dongguan, Guangdong, China

This book was typeset in Stempel Schneidler.
The illustrations were done in mixed media.

TEMPLAR BOOKS

an imprint of
Candlewick Press
99 Dover Street
Somerville, Massachusetts 02144

www.candlewick.com

PING!

ARGH!

SKIIID!

OLIVE
AND THE
BAD
MOOD

TOR FREEMAN

templar books
an imprint of Candlewick Press

O live was in a bad mood.

This was **not** a good day.

"Hello, Olive!" said Molly.
"Do you want to play
dinosaurs with me?"

"No," said Olive.
"Dinosaurs are
for babies."

"They are not!"
said Molly.

"Hello, Olive!" said Matt.
"Do you like my
new hat?"

"No," said Olive.
"It is too big and
floppy. Like
a pancake."

"No, it isn't,"
said Matt.

Olive stomped along.
Everything is silly,
she said to herself.
Look at that silly old can.
Look at that silly old flower!
There was silly old Joe.

"Hey!" said Olive.
"You're terrible
with that ball.
You couldn't
catch a cold."

"Oh, yes,
I could,"
said Joe.

Oh, boy, now Olive was
in a **really** bad mood.

And look,
here was Ziggy,
getting in
Olive's way!

"Hi, Olive," said Lola.

Olive pretended not to hear. That would show her.

"Hi, Olive!"
Lola called.

"OLIVE?"

Olive kicked
a pebble.
Look at that
silly old—

Oooh! The
candy store—
Olive's favorite.

CANDY

Olive went straight in. She bought herself a bag of giant jelly worms.

Olive walked along chewing a jelly worm.
What a lovely sunny day!
Look at that pretty green bush!
Look at those sweet little butterflies!

"And there are
all my friends!"
cried Olive.

"Hello, everyone!"
called Olive.
"Isn't it a lovely day?"

"WE'RE IN
A BAD MOOD!"
said Olive's friends.

"Well, excuse ME for breathing," said Olive.

"I only came over to see if you wanted some of this delicious candy."

The friends ate jelly worms in the sun. "See?" said Olive. "I don't know why you were all in such bad moods.

"It was lucky I was here
to cheer you up!"